MOONBEAR'S DREAM

FRANK ASCH

Aladdin Paperbacks
New York London Toronto Sydney Singapore

First Aladdin Paperbacks edition September 2002

ALADDIN PAPERBACKS
An imprint of Simon & Schuster
Children's Publishing Division
1230 Avenue of the Americas
New York, NY 10020

Also available in a Simon & Schuster Books for Young Readers hardcover edition.
Designed by Anahid Hamparian
The text of this book is set in 18-point Bookman.
The illustrations are rendered in Photoshop.
Coloration by Devin Asch in Photoshop

Printed in Hong Kong
2 4 6 8 10 9 7 5 3 1

The Library of Congress has cataloged the hardcover edition as follows:
Asch, Frank.
Moonbear's dream / Frank Asch.—1st ed.
p. cm.
Summary: When Moonbear and his friend Little Bird see a kangaroo in the backyard, they think they must be dreaming, so they do things they would not do if they were awake.
ISBN 0-689-82244-8 (hc)
[1. Bears—Fiction. 2. Birds—Fiction. 3. Dreams—Fiction. 4. Behavior—Fiction.] I. Title.
PZ7.A778Mnk 1999 [E]—dc21 98-24133 CIP AC
ISBN 0-689-85310-6 (Aladdin pbk.)

To Jan

One day a kangaroo with a joey in her pouch escaped from the zoo and wandered through Bear's yard.

"Do you see what I see?" asked Little Bird.
"I sure do," replied Bear. "But I can't believe
my eyes. It looks like something from a dream!"

"Maybe we *are* dreaming," chirped Little Bird.

"Yes, that's it!" cried Bear. "We're probably asleep in our beds right now."

"Maybe we should wake ourselves up," said Little Bird.
"Why not have some fun first?" chuckled Bear. He went inside, took down his honey jar, and started scooping out big pawfuls of honey.
"Weren't you saving that honey for winter?" asked Little Bird.

SWEET
HOME

“This is dream honey,” said Bear. “I can eat it now and it will still be here when I wake up!”

"What a great idea!" said Little Bird, and he flew to the shelf where he kept his birdseed.

SWEET
HOME

When Bear finished his honey he dropped the jar
on the floor. Crash!
"Aren't you going to clean that up?" asked Little Bird.
"Why bother?" said Bear. "When I wake up the mess
will be gone."
"That's right!" chirped Little Bird, and he pushed a vase
of flowers off the table. "Let's make a mess!"

"Let's make a *big* mess!" cried Bear.

“What fun!” whooped Little Bird. “And we don’t have to clean up! All we have to do is pinch ourselves and wake up. Then everything will be neat and tidy again!”

“I love this dream!” said Bear. “What shall we do next?”
“Let’s go for a dream swim and pick some dream berries,” chirped Little Bird.
“Okay,” agreed Bear, and they walked to the pond.

While the two friends had fun together,
the kangaroo wandered into Bear's house.

And that's where the zookeeper found her.
"Oh my!" he cried. "Look what you've done!"

ZOO
ZOO
HOME
ZOO
SEEDS
ZOO

The zookeeper quickly picked up the clutter and swept the floor. He even gave Little Bird new birdseed and fixed Bear's honey jar.
Then he tried to catch his kangaroo.

When Bear and Little Bird returned from the pond,
Bear said, “I don’t want to see that mess again.”
“Me neither!” chirped Little Bird. “Let’s wake up!”
“Okay,” said Bear, and they pinched themselves.

Then Bear opened his door.

Everything was neat and tidy.

Bear's winter honey jar was full.

And so was Little Bird's seed bag.

“Gosh, that was fun!” said Little Bird.
“But how come we’re not in our beds?”
Bear thought for a moment.

Then he said, “We must have been sleepwalking.”
“All that sleepwalking tired me out.” Little Bird yawned.
“Me too.” Bear yawned back. “Let’s take a nap.”

“Sweet dreams,” said Bear.

“Sweet dreams,” chirped Little Bird.